# Snow

D1422038

To Tijana, Milica and Stefan – my very special friends.
And very special thanks to Helen Mortimer – my editor.  M.S.

First published in the United Kingdom in 2002 by
**David Bennett Books Limited,**
an imprint of Chrysalis Books plc, 64 Brewery Road, London N7 9NT.

A member of Chrysalis Books plc

This paperback edition first published in 2002.

Text and illustrations copyright © 2002 Manya Stojic.
Manya Stojic asserts her moral right to be identified as the author and illustrator of this work.

All rights reserved. No part of this book may be reproduced, stored in a retrieval system,
or transmitted by any means, electronic, mechanical, photocopying or otherwise,
without the prior permission of the publisher.

BRITISH LIBRARY CATALOGUING-IN-PUBLICATION DATA:
A catalogue record for this book is available from the British Library.

ISBN 1 85602 471 7

Printed in Hong Kong

# Snow

written and illustrated by
## MANYA STOJIC

DAVID BENNETT BOOKS

Owl ruffled
her feathers.
"The snow is
on its way,"
she twit-twooed
wisely.

The geese were gathering.
"**The snow
is coming,**"
they sang.

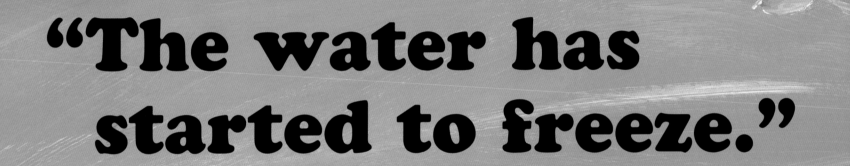

"The water has started to freeze."

"The snow
is coming,"
said Moose.
"The wind
will bring it."

"The snow is coming," Bear yawned. "Soon it will be time for my winter sleep."

Hare looked at her bunnies. "The snow is coming," she said. "Our coats are turning white."

"The snow is coming," said Fox. "The stars are covered by dark clouds."

Then it snowed. White snowflakes fell from the night sky.

# Some very big.

## Some very small.

## All very gentle.

In the morning
the forest was still.
It was covered
in a sparkling
blanket.

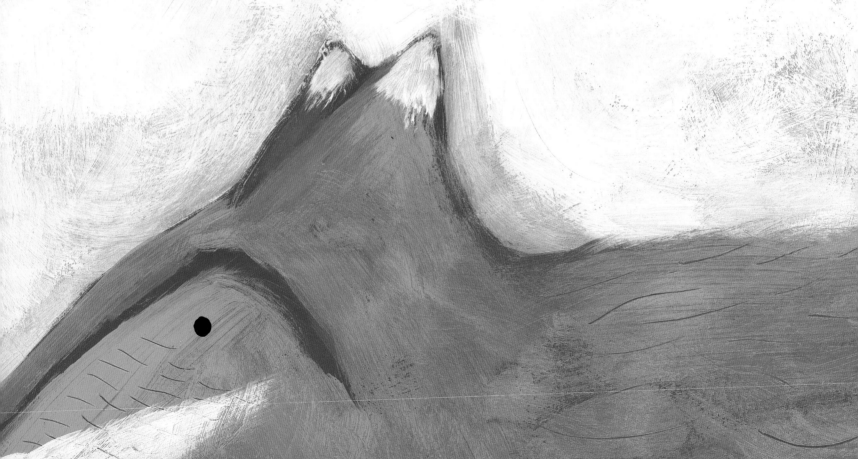

"It will be harder for me to hunt unseen," said Fox.

"Now that the snow is here."

"We are as white as we can be," giggled the bunnies. "Now that the snow is here."

"I wonder what my dreams will bring? Now that the snow is here..." mumbled Bear as he fell asleep.

"I love the fresh air!" sniffed Moose. "Now that the snow is here."

"We must fly South," said the geese.

"Now that the snow is here!"

"The snow
will stay for
many long
months..."
said Owl wisely.